Lucky Beans

by Becky Birtha
Illustrated by Nicole Tadgell

Albert Whitman & Company, Chicago, Illinois

For the J/B and Dunnaville families,
especially Herbert Marshall Birtha, and
remembering Josephine Dunnaville Birtha.
—B.B.—

Kudos and toots to all problem-solving kids!
—N.T.—

Library of Congress Cataloging-in-Publication Data

Birtha, Becky, 1948-
Lucky beans / by Becky Birtha ; illustrated by Nicole Tadgell.
p. cm.
Summary: During the Great Depression, Marshall, an African American boy, uses
lessons learned in arithmetic class and guidance from his mother to figure out how
many beans are in a jar in order to win her a new sewing machine in a contest.
ISBN 978-0-8075-4782-3
[1. Contests—Fiction. 2. Arithmetic—Fiction. 3. Family life—Fiction.
4. African Americans—Fiction. 5. Depressions—1929—Fiction. 6. United States—
History—1919-1933—Fiction.] I. Tadgell, Nicole, 1969- ill. II. Title.
PZ7.B52337Luc 2010
[E]—dc22
2009023901

The illustrations are painted in watercolor.
The design is by Lindaanne Donohoe.

For more information about Albert Whitman & Company,
please visit our web site at www.albertwhitman.com.

Cold wind ripped through Marshall Loman's old wool jacket. The snow froze his toes right through his hand-me-down boots. He ran up the steps into the steamy kitchen. "What's for dinner, Ma? I'm starving!"

"Get those boots off and hang your coat up," Ma said without looking around. "And I don't want to hear any complaints about dinner."

But Marshall had already peeked into the big pot. "Beans! Again? Aw, Ma, can't we ever have anything else?"

"Yes, it's beans again, and we're lucky to have them. So get washed on the double and then set the table."

Marshall didn't feel so lucky. The elbows of his jacket were worn almost all the way through. Dad had been out of work for months, and there was no money. The house was crowded since Aunt Minnie and Uncle Matt moved in. Now Marshall had to share a room with his little brother and sister, Tommy and Patsy.

And he was starting to hate beans.

After dinner, when Ma pulled out her mending basket, Marshall showed her his worn-out jacket.

Dad turned on the radio. "President Roosevelt's going to speak tonight," he said. "Maybe he's found a way to get America out of the mess we're in."

Marshall was halfway through his homework when the president came on the radio. He didn't understand all the big words, but he knew Mr. Roosevelt was on the poor people's side.

On the way to school the next morning, Marshall and Tommy trudged past Kaplan's Furniture Store. Whenever Marshall helped Ma carry groceries home, she would stop to look at the shining sewing machine in the window. "Only $23.95!" the sign had said. That was twenty-three dollars and ninety-five cents that Ma would never have.

Today, alongside the sewing machine was the biggest jar of beans he had ever seen. There was a different sign.

HOW MANY BEANS ARE IN THE JAR? WIN THIS BRAND NEW SEWING MACHINE!

"How many beans they got in there, Marshall?" Tommy pulled on Marshall's sleeve. "A hundred? A thousand?"

"How should I know?" Marshall answered. But he was thinking, *I know somebody who* would *know.*

On the way home, Marshall looked through the store window again. Ladies were writing on little cards of paper and pushing them through a slot into a big box.

That night, after Ma checked his homework, Marshall
told her about the contest.

The next day, when Marshall and Tommy got home, Ma said, "I went to the furniture store today." She was cooking beans again.

"Did you enter the contest?"

"Not so fast. I need a little more time to chew it over. Aren't you going to complain about having beans?" Ma joked.

Marshall shook his head. "I figure the more you know about beans, the better."

That night's homework was a page of arithmetic problems. How many cups are in a pint? Marshall knew the answer—two. How many pints are in a quart? Ma was looking over his shoulder.

"Boy, don't you know how many pints fit in a quart?" she asked. "Go down in the cellar and fetch me an empty pint jar."

In the cellar, Ma kept food she had canned from Dad's garden. There were more empty jars than full ones. Last winter, when Ma sent them to fetch something, he and Tommy would snitch a pickle from the big crock at the foot of the stairs. Now the pickle crock was empty, too.

Ma showed him how to fill up the small pint jar with water and pour it into an empty quart milk bottle to measure it. Two pints filled the quart. So four cups made a quart.

After school the next day, Marshall saw a new sign in Mr. Kaplan's window. "Only two days left to make your guess!" Kids were standing around.

"Our ma's going to win the sewing machine," Tommy piped up.

"Your ma?" Agnes, a girl in Marshall's class, whirled around to face Tommy. "They won't let your mama win. Only white ladies can win contests."

Tommy shouted back, "That's not truc!" Then he turned to Marshall. "Is it?"

Marshall grabbed his brother's hand and marched into the store. "Come on, Tommy. We're going to find out!"

"Well, young man, what can I do for you?" Mr. Kaplan said to Marshall.

"I have a question about the sewing-machine contest rules. Can anybody win? Or can only white ladies win?"

Mr. Kaplan took his glasses off and looked Marshall in the eye. "Anybody can win the contest," he said. "This is America. It will be fair."

When Marshall and Tommy got home, Ma was cooking potatoes and cabbage. But five sacks of beans sat on the kitchen table.

"Where'd all those beans come from?" Marshall asked.

"Oh, the church ladies. And neighbors. After dinner I want you boys to help me count them. But run down to the cellar now, Marshall, and fetch me a pint jar of tomatoes."

Out of habit, Marshall checked the pickle crock before starting back upstairs. Of course it was still empty—but Marshall stopped in his tracks. The pickle crock—he was sure of it—was the same size as that big jar of beans! They could count how many beans fit into the pickle crock. Then Ma would know the right number!

After dinner, Dad lugged the pickle crock up to the kitchen. They all crowded around, counting beans from the sacks and dumping them into the crock.

The last bean was number 4,341. But the 4,341 beans didn't fill much of the crock. Ma peered in. "Well," she said, "the sign did say 'guess.' I reckon that's what we'll have to do."

Then Marshall remembered something from school. His class was finished with measuring and now they were learning estimating. "It's better than guessing," Miss Dover had said. "Use what you already know to solve the problem."

Marshall said, "Ma, I know! Let's count how many beans fit in a quart jar, and how many quarts of water fill up the crock. Then we can can multiply beans times quarts to estimate the number of beans."

Ma grinned at him. "Now you're cooking with gas!" she said.

When they were finished counting and multiplying, they had the number Ma thought was right—53,280 beans.

333 beans in a cup

4 cups = 1 quart

4 x 333 = 1332 beans in a quart

4 quarts = 1 gallon

4 x 1332 = 5328 beans in a gallon

10 gallons of water fill the crock

10 x 5328 = 53,280 beans in the crock!

On Saturday morning, Mr. Kaplan's furniture store was full
of people. "Ladies and gentlemen," Mr. Kaplan announced,
"we had 327 entries—and today we have a winner! First, let's
reveal how many beans are in the jar."

He unscrewed the lid and showed the number marked inside.
"Fifty-three thousand, two hundred ninety-three!"

Marshall heard gasps and a whistle. "Holy mackerel!"
somebody said.

Marshall's heart was thumping hard. Ma's guess was so close!
Was she going to win?

Mr. Kaplan went on. "One guess was off by
only thirteen beans! And the winner, who guessed
53,280 beans, is…Mrs. Josephine Loman, from
7234 Monticello Street!"

"Ma! That's you!" Marshall threw his arms around his
mother's waist.

"Congratulations, Mrs. Loman!" Mr. Kaplan shook
Ma's hand.

After Ma won the sewing machine, everything got a little better. Ma was sewing up a storm, and getting paid for it, too. Dad got part-time work helping Mr. Kaplan with deliveries.

The only thing that wasn't so good was the other prize Ma won. That jar of beans seemed even bigger in Ma's kitchen than it had in Mr. Kaplan's store.

To Marshall, it looked like a lifetime supply!

Lucky Beans takes place during the Great Depression, which lasted in the United States from 1929, when the financial system called the stock market collapsed, until about 1939. Banks, stores, factories, and businesses closed. The Depression affected the whole country, and spread to other countries as well.

Like Marshall's dad, many people lost their jobs. In 1933, one in four workers was unemployed. For African Americans, that number was nearly two in four.

Although black and white children attended school together in northern cities, like the one where the Loman family lived, blacks and whites did not always have equal opportunities. This was long before the civil rights movement. Like Marshall, African Americans worried about facing discrimination (unfair practices) when they wanted to apply for a job, or even enter a contest.

Without jobs, people did not have money for food. Some stood in line for a free loaf of bread or got relief from the government or charities. Beans were one of the foods the government provided. They were cheap and nutritious.

Many families lost homes or farms because they couldn't pay their mortgages every month. Family members opened their homes to relatives who needed a place to stay or to boarders who could pay rent. Like Marshall's ma, people mended and repaired old things instead of throwing them out, as many people might do today.

People had fun during the Depression, too. They enjoyed newspaper comic strips about characters like "Little Orphan Annie" and listened to shows like "The Lone Ranger" on the radio. Jigsaw puzzles were a big pastime, and the game Monopoly was invented. Contests were popular.

In 1932, the American people elected Franklin Delano Roosevelt president because they hoped he could fix the economy, create jobs, and be a good leader. Roosevelt was the first president to talk directly to Americans on the radio. His broadcasts, called *Fireside Chats*, kept people's spirits up. He told Americans about the New Deal, his plan for getting people back to work.

Lucky Beans is based on the stories of my grandmother, who claimed she cooked beans by a different recipe every night during the Depression. She really did win a sewing machine in a contest by guessing how many beans were in a jar.